The
D0826608

ALSO BY SALLY GARDNER

The Magical Children series

The Boy Who Could Fly
The Boy With the Magic Numbers
The Invisible Boy
The Smallest Girl Ever
The Strongest Girl in the World

Lucy Willow

Wings & Co

Operation Bunny
Three Pickled Herrings

For older readers

The Double Shadow
I, Coriander
The Red Necklace
The Silver Blade

The Boy With the Lightning Feet

Sally Gardner

illustrated by Lydia Corry

Orion
Children's Books

To Lydia
with all my love

First published in Great Britain in 2006
by Orion Children's Books
Reissued 2013 by Orion Children's Books
a division of the Orion Publishing Group Ltd
Orion House
5 Upper St Martin's Lane
London WC2H 9EA

An Hachette UK Company

1 3 5 7 9 10 8 6 4 2

A catalogue record for this book is available from the British Library

Printed in Great Britain by
Clays Ltd, St Ives plc

ISBN 978 1 4440 1165 4

www.orionbooks.co.uk

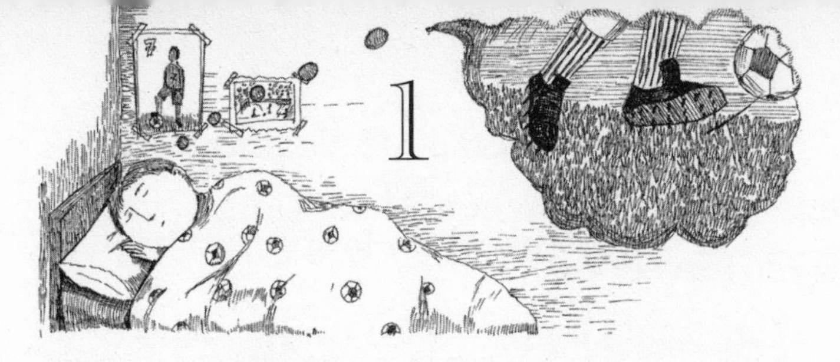

1

Timmy Twinkle was, when all's said and done, a rather chubby chap. His great love in life was football, and his great dream was to be able to play. But oh dear! He was no good at sports: in fact he believed he was useless at everything except eating.

What Timmy Twinkle didn't know was that there was magic in his toes.

Timmy hadn't always been so chubby. It started after his grandma had dropped down dead while she was out shopping for birdseed. Then, out of the blue, his mum, who'd always relied on Gran and Gramps to help her look after Timmy, decided to up sticks and start a new life in Spain. To be fair, she hadn't said that was what she was doing. She just told Gramps Twinkle that she was going for a holiday to get a tan.

'I mean, Dad,' she said to Gramps, 'I was only a kitten cat when I had Timmy, and I haven't lived yet.'

'Yep,' said Gramps, who on the whole had given up talking in sentences and only said 'yep' or 'nope' like the cowboys in the old films he and his grandson liked to watch on television.

'So you won't mind having Timmy on your own for a couple of weeks?' said Mum, turning the note on the door of Kettle's Teashop to Closed.

'Nope,' said Gramps.

'I'll be back and then we can reopen the teashop and I shall have lost my itchy feet,' said Mum.

That was that. She put on her sparkly pink top and went off to the airport with a one-way ticket.

When, after two weeks, she hadn't come back, Timmy had felt hungry. After a year of her being gone, Timmy was never not hungry. After two years, he was a very chubby little chap. He found that food filled the gap where once there had been a nice warm feeling of love and safety.

Timmy was seven then. All he had ever had from his mum was three postcards; one saying 'wish you were here, you'd love it,' the second to tell him she was working in a tapas bar and the third to say she was getting married. Timmy put all the cards in a shoebox along with the matador's hat she had sent him and a photo of her at her wedding. And every time he thought of his mum he just felt hungry.

2

The bullying had begun in Year 2, when Mickey Morris, known to the rest of the class as Mickey the Moose, joined High Hope School. It stayed pretty much the same in Year 3. Everyone was a little scared of Mickey the Moose. He was the school's best striker, a star on the football pitch. He liked to think of himself as High Hope's secret weapon.

Then it got worse. Oh boy, did it get worse after Freddy Hammer joined the class in Year 4. They ganged up big time on Timmy and made him feel very lonely and miserable.

Timmy spent his days dreaming of being anywhere except school. He dreamt all through the lessons. He began to find it hard to keep up with his work. He dreaded breaktime, when Freddy Hammer and

Mickey the Moose would push him up against the school wall and punch and kick him, then trip him up and call him Dim Tim and Fatty Batty.

Twice Timmy even bunked off school and went down to the canal near the old playing field that hadn't been used for years and was all overgrown, even though he wasn't supposed to go there on his own. He ate his packed lunch and told himself stories about scoring a goal for England. He ate the chocolate bars he'd bought with his pocket money and longed for the end of the afternoon when he could go back to Gramps and a home-made cake.

Timmy never said how bad things were at school. He couldn't because his troubles needed a bit more than Gramps's usual 'nope' and 'yep'.

It seemed that things could only get worse. But then Timmy found a photograph album, and everything changed.

3

Gramps had been a baker. He used to make all the bread and cakes for Gran's teashop. Now Gran and Timmy's mum, who also worked there, were gone, and the teashop was closed. Gramps still spent his days baking cakes. It was all he knew how to do. The trouble was there was only one customer, and that customer was Timmy Twinkle and the one thing Timmy didn't need was any more cake to eat.

Every day Timmy longed for the moment when he would open the front door and a waft of baking would wrap itself round him. Gramps would serve tea: home-made scones with lashings of whipped cream and his own strawberry jam, followed by a sponge cake that seemed filled with love and iced with hope.

They never said much, Gramps and Timmy. Even Sheriff the parrot was silent. He used to be the life and soul of the teashop, greeting the customers with 'Howdy-do, cowboy? Have you tied up your horse?' which made everyone laugh. But he too had given up talking after Gran's funeral and now refused to croak a word.

'Perhaps he'd start talking if we opened the teashop again,' said Timmy.

'Yep,' said Gramps.

Still, the teashop stayed closed. Sheriff gave up coming into the lounge of an evening and sitting on Gramps's shoulder to watch the old cowboy movies. Instead, he spent most of his time on his perch in the empty shop with his head under his wing.

'Do you think he's all right?' asked Timmy, when Sheriff's feathers began to fall out.

'Nope,' said Gramps.

'He looks more like a plucked chicken than a parrot,' said Timmy.

'Yep,' said Gramps.

'Do you think he should go to the vet?' asked Timmy.

'Yep,' said Gramps, and he put Sheriff in his cage and set off to town in his Morris Minor.

That was when Timmy spotted it, the old photograph album that the birdcage had been sitting on.

Its cover had got all dusty and was peeling apart, but inside the pictures were as good as new. They were all of the same young man. There were pictures of him with a handlebar moustache, dressed in

old-fashioned clothes, with his leather lace-up boots resting on a football. The one Timmy liked best was of him being carried on the shoulders of his team-mates. He had a big beaming smile across his face and was holding up a huge cup. Underneath was written 'Lytham St Anne's Champion League Winner 1912.'

Gramps returned with Sheriff. The parrot was not in a good mood and sulked on his perch.

'Is he all right now?' asked Timmy.

'Yep. Nope,' replied Gramps. He put the cage back where it belonged and sat down in his favourite armchair. For some reason the cage wobbled unsteadily on the coffee table. Gramps looked at it, trying to figure out what was wrong.

'I think you need to put this under it,' said Timmy, showing Gramps the photo album.

'Yep,' said Gramps.

'I've been looking at it,' said Timmy. 'Can I keep it out? It's all football pictures.'

'Yep,' replied Gramps, finding an old Army and Navy catalogue to use instead.

'Who's this, Gramps?' asked Timmy, showing Gramps the picture of the young man. 'Is he someone important?'

Gramps put on his glasses and looked at the photo. 'Yep,' he said. Timmy felt a flutter of excitement in his tummy.

'Do you know him, then?' asked Timmy.

'Nope,' said Gramps.

'I wish I knew who he was,' said Timmy, staring at the photo album and not expecting an answer. He was used to Gramps not talking. He knew he would just have to ask some more simple 'yep' and 'nope' questions if he wanted to find out who the man in the sepia photo was.

That was when Gramps spoke, which was something he hadn't done for a very long time. He said, 'He was Gran's Great-Great Uncle Vernon. Everyone called him Twinkletoes.'

Timmy was amazed. That, he thought, was more than a few words. That was a whole sentence.

4

The letter arrived that Saturday morning. Gramps was in his dressing gown making tea and toast.

'I got a letter,' said Gramps.

Timmy stared at his Gramps. He still wasn't used to hearing him say more than 'nope' and 'yep'. He wasn't sure if he liked it better when Gramps talked, for he had a feeling he was in trouble.

'What's the letter about?' he asked nervously.

Gramps put the tea and toast on the table and sat down. He pulled the letter out of his pocket. The words High Hope School were written clearly on the top, and Timmy's heart sank.

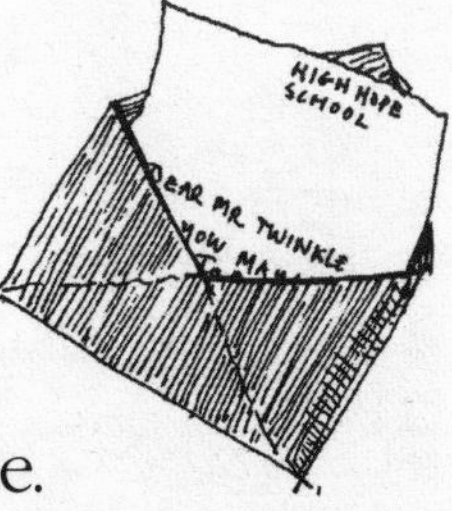

'You've missed school twice. What's up, lad?'

Timmy stirred his tea and kept his eyes on the check tablecloth. And felt hungry.

'I don't mind what it is that's bothering you, lad,' said Gramps. 'Better out than in. So take your time but tell the truth.'

It took Timmy quite a while and quite a few rounds of toast to tell Gramps all that was wrong. He told him about the bullying, about Mickey the Moose and Freddy Hammer, about being laughed at and called names. Gramps listened.

'You won't go telling my teacher, will you? If Mickey the Moose knew I'd said anything, it would be even worse,' said Timmy.

Gramps put an arm around his grandson. Timmy felt hot, angry tears roll down his cheeks.

'Nay, lad,' said Gramps. 'But I'll tell you this for nowt; bullies are always cowards. Stand up to a bully and you'll find a mouse in lion's clothes.'

Gramps handed Timmy a big white handkerchief.

'You know that photo album you found?'

Timmy blew his nose and nodded.

'Well,' said Gramps, stirring the sugar in his tea. 'Great-Great Uncle Vernon was one of the finest strikers in the North of England. He scored more goals than I've baked cakes. He went off to fight in the First World War. He was a gunner, never came home. I took your gran to see his grave in France where he fell. He was only a youngster. A terrible waste.'

Gramps took a swig of his tea. Then he said, 'I found another picture of the lad.

I thought you might like to take a look at it.' He produced a photo framed in a gilt-edged card, and there was a picture of a lad a little older than Timmy.

Timmy looked at it. Then he looked at it again. 'He's really chubby, like me,' he said.

'Yep,' said Gramps. 'And another thing, lad. He was bullied at school something rotten, just like you.'

'What made it stop?' asked Timmy.

'Football,' said Gramps, 'and his twinkle toes.'

And for the first time in ages, Timmy thought he saw a ray of light at the end of a very long tunnel. If Gran's Great-Great Uncle Vernon could do it, then so could Timmy Twinkle.

5

Timmy's chance came sooner than he expected. Donald McNab had broken his ankle skateboarding and was unable to play in the next school match. Mr Daniels, the sports teacher, had put a notice up saying he was looking for a replacement and anyone interested should come to his office in break.

'What are you doing here?' said Mickey the Moose, pushing Timmy up against the wall in the school corridor. 'Think you can replace Donald McNab? What a joke.'

There was a guffaw from the other boys and they all started to join in, pushing and prodding at Timmy. Timmy had learned from long, bitter experience that it wasn't worth replying.

Mr Daniels came out of his office. 'Mickey, what are you doing?'

'Nothing, sir,' said Mickey. 'Just talking to Timmy Twinkle.'

There was a snigger from the group of boys.

'What's so funny about that?' asked Mr Daniels.

'Nothing, sir,' said Freddy Hammer. 'It's just that he ain't football material, is he, sir?'

'And what makes you such an expert, Hammer?' snapped Mr Daniels. 'If you want to stay on the team, this is not the way to go about it.'

As Timmy put on his sports kit, he felt that they might all be right. Why, only a term ago it had fitted, but now the elastic round his middle was stretched to breaking point and his tummy flopped over his shorts. He was just about to give up when Mr Daniels shouted, 'Come on, Twinkle. We're waiting for you.'

Timmy walked out on to the playing field. Everyone laughed.

'Hey Fatty! You need a girly bra.'

'Where's your knees? Oh diddums. They've gone and got lost.'

Mr Daniels blew his whistle. 'No more talking. For now we're just going to chase the ball.'

It was hopeless. Timmy could hardly run. He puffed and panted after the ball.

The other boys made sure that he never got it.

Mickey the Moose tripped him up. Timmy fell and was immediately covered in mud.

'Hey, piggy,' said Freddy Hammer, 'don't bother to get up. You belong down there.'

Mr Daniels blew his whistle loudly and

took the ball from Mickey.

'Any more fouls from you,' he said, 'and I'll tell you this for nothing, you won't be on my team.'

'Yeah, sir,' said Mickey.

Mr Daniels gave the ball to Timmy.

'Just kick it,' he said, 'at least once.'

What Timmy did then shocked everyone on the pitch. He was well away from the goal but he kicked the ball straight into it. Well, that was the thing. It wasn't straight. Timmy curved the ball into the goal, just like Beckham.

Everyone stood stock still and stared in amazement.

'It's a fluke, sir!' said Mickey.

'Beginner's luck!' said Freddy Hammer.

Mr Daniels blew his whistle and gave the ball back to Timmy.

'OK, lad, let's see if you can do that again.'

And blow Mr Daniels down, Timmy did.

Mr Daniels couldn't remember seeing any pupil do that before. He decided to give the boy a chance. When the football team was read out, Timmy Twinkle's name was on the substitutes list.

As Gramps said, 'You've got to start somewhere, lad, and being on the team, even as a substitute, is as good a start as any.'

6

All this happened before the summer holidays. However, although Timmy was on the team he never once got to play whereas the other two substitutes were used all the time. Timmy was left sitting on the bench to watch the game and to look after the water bottles, covered in everyone's T-shirts.

'Do you know what you are?' said Freddy Hammer. 'A nothing. You're just a clothes horse. You'll never be a footballer.'

Still Timmy sat and watched, match after match. In his mind he knew how he would

have kicked the ball in every game. He also knew that he was never going to be asked to play.

'If I were you,' said Mickey the Moose, 'I wouldn't bother next term, fat boy. Because the bench ain't going to be able to hold that weight much longer.'

Timmy had had enough of all those hurtful words. He spoke to Mr Daniels. He said that he didn't want to be on the team any more.

'Hang on a minute,' said Mr Daniels.

Timmy didn't. He just turned and walked away. There had been too many minutes that had added themselves up into hours and hours of bullying. He had hung on for far too long.

Timmy was in tears as he walked back along the canal. He was surprised to see a young lad standing in front of him on the towpath, holding a football. He looked as if he was waiting for someone.

It was a warm day, and through Timmy's tears the lad glimmered in a heat haze. He kept his head down, not wishing to make eye contact, and walked quickly past. After all, he was still wearing his football kit and he knew he looked a prat.

He waited for the lad to shout out, 'Yo-ho, you're a big girl's blouse, you are,' but what he actually said made Timmy stop in his tracks.

'Eh, lad, want to play some footie?'

Timmy looked up and saw that he was dressed most oddly. He had a flat cap, a knitted sweater, long shorts with thick socks and odd-looking leather boots. He remembered Gramps saying that they had been filming down by the canal.

'Are you an actor?' asked Timmy. The lad seemed not to hear. He just said, 'Come on,' as if he had known Timmy all his life, and walked towards the old playing field. Timmy hesitated, remembering Gramps's instructions about never talking to strangers. The lad looked OK though, as if he really did want to play football, so after a moment Timmy followed.

At first Timmy hardly knew the old playing field, for it was completely changed. It had the greenest grass, like velvet, cut short and marked out like a proper football pitch.

The lad put the football down. It was then that Timmy realised that it was just like the one in the picture of Great-Great Uncle Vernon in the photo album. Come to think of it, the clothes were the same, too. He was about to ask what the film was when the lad started to kick the football.

Timmy watched amazed as he ran with the ball, making it dance and come back to him. He kicked it towards Timmy.

'Why aren't you joining in?'

'I can't. I'm no good,' said Timmy.

'Nay,' the lad replied, 'you can be as good as me. Come on, I'll show you. It's all in the toes.'

That afternoon Timmy felt lean and light and hungry, not for food but for playing the beautiful game. He was able to run without losing his breath. He watched and learnt and the unkind world slipped away, and all there was was football.

He had no idea how long they played.

By the time they stopped, the shadows had grown longer and the grass had turned golden in the evening light.

As they walked back towards the towpath, the lad said, 'You could be better than me, live longer, be a real star, you know. You have the gift. You have lightning in your feet.'

'Do you really think so?' asked Timmy eagerly. 'Will you teach me some more? Will you come again tomorrow? What's your name? Mine's Timmy Twinkle.'

'I know that,' said the lad, and he vanished into the twilight.

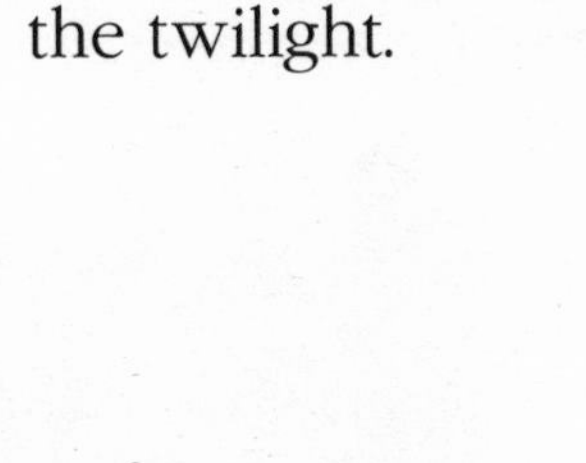

7

Timmy told Gramps about taking himself off the football team, and about the strange lad he had met down by the canal.

'What do you think?' asked Timmy.

'I think it's a pity you've given up, but I'm glad you met the lad,' said Gramps.

'Do you think he was an actor?' asked Timmy.

'Does it matter?' asked Gramps.

The next day Gramps was called in to see Mr Peters, the headmaster.

'Everything all right at home?' asked Mr Peters.

'It's been better,' said Gramps.

'I'm sorry,' said Mr Peters. 'I heard about your wife's death and about Tracy going off to Spain.

Is Timmy's father around?'

Gramps laughed. 'Nope. He was only a youngster when they had Timmy. Both of them had heads full of air. Neither knew nowt about much. He lives in Cornwall now, drives a lorry. Can't say we keep in touch.'

'A tricky thing when teenagers have babies,' said Mr Peters.

'Yep,' said Gramps.

'Mr Daniels, the sports teacher, tells me that Timmy has taken himself off the football team.'

'Yep,' said Gramps.

'It's a terrible pity. According to Mr Daniels, the boy has real flair,' said Mr Peters.

'Then perhaps you might like to ask him to play,' said Gramps, 'instead of sticking him on the end of the bench week after week.'

'The trouble is, Mr Twinkle,' said Mr Peters, 'Timmy is rather overweight. He is very good at getting the ball into the goal, but sadly that's not enough. The boy needs to be able to run.'

'Chicken and egg,' said Gramps, getting up.

'Excuse me?' said Mr Peters. 'What exactly do you mean?'

'If the lad don't ever get to play, how is he going to get fitter?' said Gramps.

'Couldn't you get him to lose some weight over the school holidays?' said Mr Peters. 'Then he could try again next term.'

'That'll be up to the lad,' said Gramps.

Gramps walked home instead of taking the bus. On the way, he stopped off at the local bookshop and flicked through all the cookbooks until he found what he wanted. Then he sat in a café reading and making a list.

That afternoon when Timmy got home there was no lovely smell of baking wafting out to greet him, just the good wholesome smell of a chicken roasting. It was most strange that Gramps was cooking anything other than cakes.

'What's going on?' asked Timmy.

'This, me lad,' said Gramps, 'is the start of us eating better. Footballers have to be fit and you won't get fit by eating my chocolate cake, nay, no matter how good it is.'

They ate their supper together in silence. It wasn't that it didn't taste good. It just didn't seem to fill Timmy up like the chocolate cake had done.

'Cat got your tongue?' asked Gramps.

'You know that boy I told you about?'

said Timmy, trying hard not to think about scones with lashings of whipped cream and jam.

'Yep,' said Gramps.

'I went down to the canal today but he wasn't there and I can't find where it was we played. Where do you think they're filming?'

'I don't know, lad,' said Gramps.

'Perhaps if we could find out, I could get to see him again.'

'Nay,' said Gramps quietly. 'I'm not saying it is, and I'm not saying it's not, but when I was a lad I felt very close to Great-Great

Uncle Vernon, even though he was dead by the time I was born.'

'What do you mean?' asked Timmy.

'I used to find that in time of need Great-Great Uncle Vernon would be there.'

'But you said he was dead,' said Timmy.

'Yep, that's what I said,' said Gramps.

Timmy stared at him, not quite sure if he understood. For the lad he had played football with the day before was real. He was no ghost. That was impossible.

9

Small changes bring about bigger changes and Gramps talking again was to be the start of something altogether bigger. He could talk on the phone now, a thing he hadn't done for years. So when May, his and Gran's old schoolfriend, called to say that she was visiting England from the States and wanted to see Gramps, he invited her to come and stay for the whole summer.

The minute he put the phone down, Gramps said, 'Eh, lad, what have I done?' and became all nervous. But then Timmy and Gramps spent a happy weekend together painting the spare room, and not long after that a taxi drew up outside the teashop and May got out.

Timmy had never seen his Gramps look so chuffed, and May was nothing like he had imagined. He had thought she would

be a sweet old lady wearing sweet old lady clothes bought from jumble sales, like Gran's. May wore nothing of the sort. She looked really good. She had fancy trainers on. Her hair was tied up in a scarf and she had some very large beads round her neck that looked like small cherry tomatoes. She didn't try to kiss Timmy or anything awful like that and she had brought him some cool CDs as a present.

Sheriff, who had not taken much interest in anything for ages, cheered up the minute May arrived and flew round the teashop squawking loudly, 'Howdy-do, howdy-do.'

They sat in the empty teashop and had one of Gramps's special teas. He had spent ages baking a magnificent chocolate cake. May said it was the best she had ever tasted. 'Why, Charlie Twinkle, you could make a fortune selling these,' she said.

'What do you want to do while you're here?' asked Gramps, still a bit nervous.

'I want to see Stratford-upon-Avon, the Tower of London, Brighton and heaps more. And I'd like to go back to Lytham St Anne's and see where you and I and Annie went to school.'

Timmy looked at Gramps and Gramps nodded. 'It'll be a right pleasure to take you there,' he said.

'Well,' said May, 'that is mighty kind of you. In that case you must let me do something for you in return.'

'Nope,' said Gramps, looking up over his paper. 'You're a guest and guests do nowt.'

May laughed.

'You know what they say about guests and fish, don't you?'

'What?' asked Timmy.

'That guests, like fish, go off after three days.'

Gramps smiled.

'So,' May went on, 'if this is going to work, Charlie Twinkle, I want to be thought of as part of the family.'

And that settled it.

Over the following days Timmy got to know and like May. He told her all about school and football, about being bullied and about the lad he met by the canal. May, just like Gramps, listened and thought. And one evening over tea she came up with a plan.

'Now, there's something not right here, and this is what we're going to do,' announced May.

Gramps looked worried.

'You've let yourself go, Charlie Twinkle. Just look at you! When you got married to Annie, you were full of zip.'

'Eh, that were a lifetime ago, lass,' said Gramps.

'No excuses,' said May. 'And it's not only you. There's Timmy.'

'What about me?' asked Timmy.

'He told me about the football team,' said May to Gramps. 'Charlie, we've got to help him. By the end of the summer, he's got to be ready to get on to the team. He's got to thin down and get fit.'

'We've been trying to eat better,' said Timmy. 'Gramps hardly ever bakes cakes now.'

'That's good, but you need exercise!' said May. 'Exercise and more exercise! We'll put you on a training schedule. Back home, I take Keep Fit classes so while I'm here I want you to think of me as your personal trainer. Hey, it'll be fun, I promise you.'

Timmy wasn't too sure about that. It all sounded like very hard work to him.

May laughed. 'Come on guys, this isn't a punishment. This is going to be the making of Timmy Twinkle.'

10

School was over and the summer holidays had begun. Every morning the three of them ate fruit and cereal, went swimming and did May's work-out plan. Timmy thought he'd hate it. He was surprised to find that he didn't.

'Just take your time and build up slowly,' May advised him.

The funny thing was that Timmy found that the more he did, the less he felt like a sofa, and the less he felt like a sofa the happier he became. And the happier he became, the less he felt like eating four slices of chocolate cake rather than one.

That summer was the best he could remember. Every weekend they took off in Gramps's Morris Minor. Even Sheriff was allowed to come. May wouldn't hear of him being left in the pet shop while they were away.

They visited Stonehenge, Land's End, Brighton Pavilion. They went to Stratford and fed the swans and visited Anne Hathaway's Cottage. They walked on Hadrian's Wall. And they went to Lytham St Anne's to see the school Gramps, Gran and May had been to, and Timmy saw a plaque in the school corridor with Great-

Great Uncle Vernon's name there, saying he had been killed in the First World War.

On weekdays they all got up early. Timmy went running before breakfast, followed by Gramps on his bike shouting, 'Go for it, lad.' He did press-ups and sit-ups

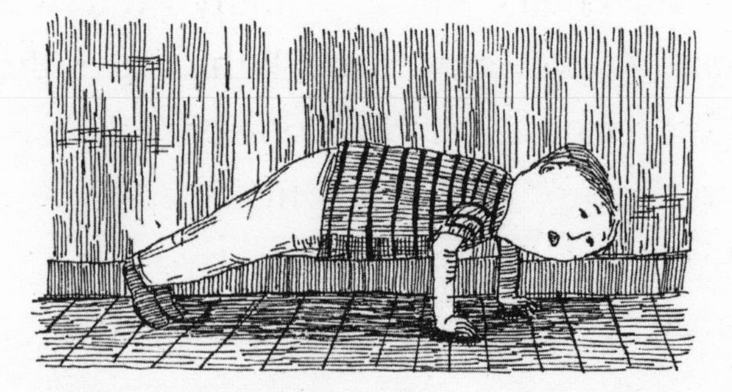

until his tummy hurt. He went swimming and played tennis. Gramps insisted on showing him and May how to play bowls. And in every spare moment Timmy kicked a football

round the garden, until the ball felt almost attached to him.

May told Timmy not to bother standing on the scales. 'Just do it on how it feels. And if your clothes start getting too big for you, it's working.'

By the end of August, Timmy's wall was covered in postcards from all the places they had been to and his trousers were falling down. Gramps had to pull his belt in too.

'I think it's about time you two got yourselves some new clothes instead of looking like a couple of scarecrows,' said May.

Timmy thought that before they went shopping he and Gramps were like two caterpillars. Now, in their new outfits, they had turned into butterflies. Gramps looked a different person and Timmy had a whole new wardrobe as well as some great new football boots. May even took him to the barber's and he had a proper haircut instead of Gramps's usual pudding basin cut.

'You look swell,' said May, giving Timmy a big hug. 'When you get back to school, you show them what you can do. Don't let those bullies get you down.'

'I won't. But you'll be here to see me play, won't you?' asked Timmy.

May sipped her herbal tea. 'I love being here with you guys. Why, it's been the best. But hey, honey, time's up.'

'Meaning?' asked Timmy.

'Meaning that I have to go home. I have an apartment and work waiting for me.'

Timmy felt once more that the world had a hole in it, a hole that only a lot of jam doughnuts would fill.

'Hey, don't look so sad,' said May.

'What will we do without you?' asked Timmy, feeling as near to tears as he had done for ages. 'You can't go. Gramps might stop talking again, like he did after Gran went.'

'Honey,' replied May, 'he won't, believe me.'

'I might give up working out,' said Timmy desperately.

'No, you won't, Timmy Twinkle. You can do this.'

Gramps too looked miserable and Sheriff sat mournfully on his perch with his head hidden under his wing.

'Oh stop it, all of you,' said May, 'you're making me feel really bad.'

'Eh, stay then, lass,' said Gramps, 'stay and help me run the teashop. You could do Keep Fit classes upstairs and, and –'

'I can't, Charlie Twinkle,' said May. 'I really have to go back. But I'll call. And I don't want to hear that things have gone back to their old ways. You promise me?'

Gramps and Timmy both promised.

11

By the time the autumn term came round, Timmy was as brown as a button and in good shape. So much so that when he arrived at school Mickey Morris and Freddy Hammer didn't know him.

'Are you a new boy?' asked Freddy Hammer.

'Nope,' said Timmy.

Mickey looked fed up when he recognised Timmy, for he had liked it better when he had been really chubby. There had been more to pick on. Now Timmy Twinkle looked like every other boy in the class. He sighed. Then he and Freddy caught sight of the real new boy and went for him like a couple of cats that had got a whiff of a mouse.

Jason Dine was taller than all the other boys and girls in his class. He looked a bit like a pencil, a fact that Freddy Hammer and Mickey the Moose were quick to catch on to.

'What's the weather like up there?' asked Freddy Hammer.

'Do you need a pencil sharpener? Get the point?' sneered Mickey.

Jason Dine said nothing, just kept his head down and his shoulders hunched. Straight away Timmy recognised a fellow sufferer. This, he thought to himself, wasn't the first school that Jason Dine had been bullied at.

The rest of the class were relieved to see that Mickey and Freddy had found someone else to pick on. They didn't care who it was as long as it wasn't them. Timmy felt dread wrap itself around him as he saw the new boy squirm with misery.

At break Jason Dine went and hid as far away from his classmates as possible. Timmy found him round the back of the art block.

'Hello,' he said.

'I wouldn't bother if I were you,' said Jason, kicking at a pebble.

'Come again?' said Timmy.

'I know you've been told by the teacher to be nice to the new boy,' said Jason. 'Don't worry, go and join your friends. It don't bother me.'

'Those? My friends!' said Timmy. 'You must be joking. And just for the record, the teacher didn't say anything to me. I don't have a friend here and I thought . . .' He stopped and let out a sigh. 'It doesn't matter,' said Timmy, walking away.

'Wait,' called Jason. 'I'm sorry. I would like to be your friend.'

'OK, then,' said Timmy.

It turned out that Timmy and Jason had a lot more in common than they thought. They were both mad about football. Both had lost their mums. Jason's had left him when he was five and gone off and married a car salesman. He wasn't sure where she was.

'It's just me and me dad now,' he said as they sat eating their tea with Gramps at Timmy's house. 'We moved this way because of Dad's work.' He paused. 'Well, more for me to start in a new school, I suppose. We needn't have bothered. Nothing's going to change.'

'Eh, that's not the way to look at it, lad,' said Gramps. 'Look, you've made a friend already.'

'Two,' squawked Sheriff.

Everyone turned round in surprise as Sheriff flew from his perch and landed on Jason's head.

'Oh, get off, you daft bird,' said Gramps.

But Sheriff wouldn't budge.

'Howdy-do,' he said looking very pleased with himself.

Jason and Timmy burst out laughing. They watched Gramps chase Sheriff round the tearoom, only for the parrot to land on Jason's head again.

'He doesn't do that for everyone,' said Gramps, catching his breath. 'Only family, so you're honoured.'

'I'm well chuffed,' said Jason. 'And I like you too, Sheriff,' he said, reaching up and stroking the parrot's head. 'Thanks for having me.'

'Any time, lad,' said Gramps. 'And don't you forget, you've three new friends now. That's proof that things do change.'

Timmy waved Jason goodbye and felt that this term was going to be all right after all.

12

'Isn't it daft,' said Timmy to Jason one afternoon as they were kicking a ball around the playing field. 'You know that saying "sticks and stones can break my bones but words can never hurt me."'

'Yes,' said Jason. 'I do and it stinks. It's what Dad says all the time.'

'Well, it's wrong, that's for sure,' said Timmy. 'All those words that Mickey the Moose and Freddy the Hammer used hurt a lot. They made my life gross.'

'Snap,' said Jason. 'Why do you think they do it?'

'Gramps says it's because they're cowards,' said Timmy. 'He says they're mice dressed in lions' clothes and that behind every bully is another bully.'

'Who starts it? That's what I'd like to know,' said Jason.

'Tell you what, there's two of us now and that's a whole lot better than one,' said Timmy.

It was this that gave the boys the courage they needed to go for the trials for the school's Under Ten Football Team, even though there were fifteen boys competing for eight places.

'Not you again,' said Mickey. 'You may be thinner but underneath that skin you'll always be a fat boy.' And he pushed Timmy out of the way as Freddy Hammer charged in front of them.

'Oh, look what we have here. A sad load

of chiefs you are. Pencil head and fat boy,' said Freddy Hammer, giggling.

Timmy said nothing. Neither did Jason. They both knew that words would just make it worse. They changed into their sports kit and ran on to the field to join the others.

Mr Daniels blew his whistle and threw in the ball.

'Call that fast, you no-hoper,' shouted Freddy as Mickey tripped Timmy up on purpose, then rushed over and tackled Jason, bringing him to the ground too. Mr Daniels blew his whistle.

'You two, any more of that kind of fouling and you'll be off the team. Get me?'

'Yes sir,' said Freddy and Mickey together.

In that moment something in Timmy clicked, like a light being turned on in a dark room. He stood up and it seemed that everyone on the pitch had disappeared. He rubbed his eyes. There next to him was the lad he had met by the canal.

'Timmy Twinkle, I've told you already. You've got lightning in your feet. Use it,' said the lad. 'Just as I showed you. Use it,' he said again, fading away.

The whistle blew again. Timmy blinked. He must be seeing things. There was no sign of the lad anywhere. He stared down at his football boots. They seemed to glow against the turf. Was this what the lad meant?

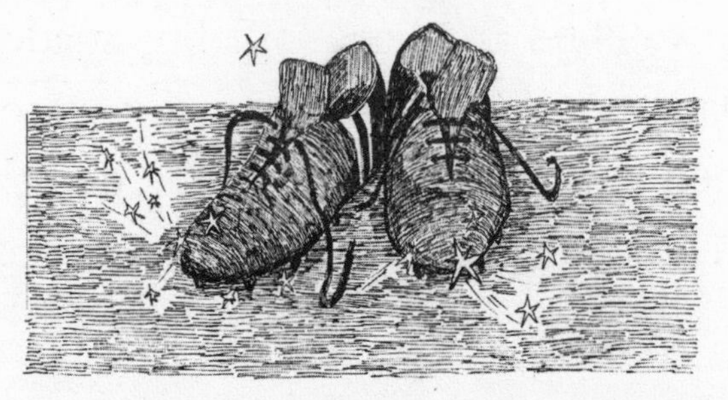

Mr Daniels had been teaching for more years than he cared to remember, and his dream had always been to find a great young player. There had been Sam Redburn, but he was too small altogether, got as far as the trials at Tottenham and hadn't made it. He told Mr Daniels afterwards that he wanted to be a jockey, not a footballer. That was right at the beginning of Mr Daniels' teaching career. Now, nearing the end, he had all but given up the idea of ever finding a David Beckham or a Wayne Rooney.

Fantasy football was all he had to dream about these days. That was until this afternoon.

He watched amazed as the boy made the ball dance and dive for him as if it were attached by invisible strings. Was this really Timmy Twinkle, the chubby lad who last term had lost his breath just running on to the football pitch? Here he was, faster than the wind. No one could stop him. And the way he kicked that ball, the power in it was astonishing! A word came to his mind, and that word was magical.

Mickey Morris and Freddy Hammer were the only two to challenge him, and that was by cheating. Mr Daniels blew his whistle just before the boys could do any damage to what he now thought of as his star player. He ordered Mickey and Freddy off the pitch and made them sit on the sub bench and watch.

When practice was over the boys walked back to the changing room. For once Mickey and Freddy were lost for words. Timmy was fantastic, but it stuck in their throats to admit it.

Mr Daniels read out the team.

'Fergus McNab, captain; Jason Dine, goalie; Alan Croft, mid-fielder; Charlie Holdgate, defender; Donald McNab, defender; Timmy Twinkle, striker.'

There was silence in the changing room. You could have heard a pin drop.

'That's all the players I'm going to announce for now,' said Mr Daniels, getting off the bench he'd been standing on. 'I'm still thinking about the rest of the team.'

'But sir,' said the boys, all talking together. 'That's not fair. Why should they know and not us?'

'Quiet,' said Mr Daniels. 'Freddy Hammer and Mickey Morris, I want to see you both in my office.'

The two boys followed Mr Daniels, glowering at the chosen few. They stood before him with a sullen look on their faces.

'I'll tell you this for nothing, keep looking like that and those expressions might just stick to your faces forever,' said Mr Daniels.

'It's not fair, sir,' said Mickey, 'I'm always on the team. I'm the best striker this school's ever had.'

'Best at what, exactly?' asked Mr Daniels. 'Tripping up your team-mates or playing football?' Then, before Mickey could say another word, he said, 'This is the deal.' And he told them what he expected of them if they wanted to be on his team.

'Otherwise,' he said menacingly, 'it will be you two sitting on the sub bench. Do I make myself clear?'

For once Mickey the Moose felt worried, very worried indeed.

14

It was Saturday, the first match of the season, and after breakfast, Gramps said, 'I've a surprise for you.'

'What?' asked Timmy.

'I'm not telling,' said Gramps, tickling him. 'You'll just have to wait until after the game.'

And however much Timmy pleaded, he wouldn't say another word.

Timmy had been looking forward to the Saturday match all week but now the day was here he felt his insides were full of jumping frogs. He couldn't even eat his cereal, he felt so nervous.

'I feel all wobbly, Gramps,' said Timmy.

'So you should, lad,' said Gramps. 'It'd be odd if you didn't. Everyone gets nervous before a game.'

For the last three weeks Mr Daniels had been working the team really hard, pushing them on, and today was the big day. They were going to play Auburn School, who had won the Cup last year. The sun shone and the field was dry. If anything it was in need of rain. All the parents, including Gramps, were there, and the Auburn School team looked very smart in their sponsored football kit. They had 'Mockers Marshmallows' stamped on their shirts, and wore matching socks.

It would be true to say that the High Hope team's kit looked a little sad.

'It's not about what we wear,' said Mr Daniels. 'It's the way that we play that matters. Go out there, boys and show them what you've got.'

15

In the first ten minutes High Hope School showed what they'd got all right, which wasn't a lot. Auburn Juniors were making mincemeat of them. It looked as if the match would be a walkover. Auburn quickly scored one goal, then another. The shouts from the parents were deafening and one voice in the crowd seemed to boom above the rest. It was so loud that Timmy turned round to see who it belonged to. There, sitting in a folding chair, was a mountain of a man with the reddest of faces.

It hadn't occurred to Timmy that noise could be a problem. He couldn't hear himself think, let alone feel his toes. Mickey Morris charged forward and managed to get the ball back from the defenders. Timmy ran down the side to get in position for Mickey to pass the ball to him so he could strike it into the goal. As he stood poised, a voice boomed out, 'What are you waiting for? For Christmas' sakes, score!'

'Pass it!' shouted Mr Daniels from the sidelines, 'pass it to Timmy.'

Mickey didn't. Instead he aimed and kicked, sending the ball high over the goal posts. A groan went up from the High Hope parents and players.

'Call that a shot!' shouted the man in the folding chair. 'A baby could have scored from that distance, you babbling fool!'

He'd gone even redder in the face, so that his veins stood out like motorways on a map of Britain, and when the ref went over and told him to be quiet, it had no effect at all.

16

After that, for some reason Timmy couldn't understand, Mickey seemed determined to play a one-boy game. If he got the ball he wouldn't pass it. If Freddy Hammer got the ball he'd pass it right over to Mickey, who went for the goal as if his life depended on it and then missed the very few chances there were of scoring.

All Mr Daniels' teaching had fallen apart. The team was a mess. The game looked all over bar the shouting, and the man in the folding chair was doing most of that.

Timmy saw that if he didn't do something this game would be lost. Spurred on, he found his feet and went for it. He got

the ball off Mickey and showed the team what could be done. Almost immediately, he scored his first goal, shortly followed by a second.

Now Mickey started to play better. He stopped hogging the ball and began passing it. It was three minutes from the end and all they needed was one more goal.

Mickey managed to get the ball from an Auburn player, deep in his own half. It was dangerously close to their home goal. Jason had his eye on the ball, sure that Mickey would kick it towards him.

At that point the mountain of a man stood up, the folding chair stuck to his backside, and charged towards the pitch.

'What blooming use are you if you can't even score a goal!' he yelled.

Startled, Mickey lost his concentration and accidentally kicked the ball sideways into the path of an Auburn player who booted it into the back of the net. The final whistle blew. Auburn School had won by one goal.

'You numbskull, you piece of useless meat!' shouted the mountain, and he stood there waving his arms whilst a stout lady tried to free the chair from his backside.

Mickey sprinted for the changing rooms as fast as his legs would carry him. Timmy Twinkle and the rest of the team watched in disbelief as the stout lady shouted, 'Oh for goodness sake, Ted, will you stay still! I can't get this blasted thing off whilst you're running about!'

It was like something out of a comedy film except no one was laughing. It was left to poor Mr Daniels to try to calm the man down and get him separated from the folding chair.

Mickey was hiding behind a locker in the changing room, looking really scared.

'Has he gone?' he asked.

'Mr Daniels is out there trying to sort him out. And by the way, thanks for losing the match,' said Fergus McNab, walking away in disgust.

'Who is he?' asked Timmy.

'What's it to you?' said Mickey, looking as near to tears as Timmy had ever seen him.

'Nothing,' said Timmy. 'It's just that he ruined the game for us, that's all.'

Mickey looked down at his feet and said something in a mumbled kind of whisper. It took Timmy a few moments to realise what he had heard, then it sank in. The largest and scariest man he'd ever seen was Mickey the Moose's dad.

17

Gramps whistled all the way home.

'Why are you in such a good mood when we lost the game?' asked Timmy.

'Two things,' said Gramps. 'First, I have a star of a grandson who has twinkle toes if ever I saw them. And second . . .' Here he smiled.

'Yes?' said Timmy.

'The second,' said Gramps mysteriously, 'is waiting at home.'

'It's the surprise!' said Timmy. He'd forgotten all about it.

Timmy walked a bit faster, then a bit slower, and then he stopped altogether.

'Gramps,' he asked, 'is it Mum?'

The smile faded from Gramps's face.

'Oh no lad, oh dear no. Is that a huge disappointment?'

'No,' said Timmy. 'I don't want to be

rude or anything but I don't want to live in Spain. I don't want to leave you.'

'Good. That's what I thought,' said Gramps, smiling again.

'It's not that I don't love Mum,' said Timmy.

'Never thought that,' said Gramps. 'Not for a moment.'

They walked up the road to the house. Outside, a lady on a ladder was putting a lick of paint to the shopfront. Timmy looked up.

'So we're having the teashop painted,' he said.

'Well, yes, but that's not the surprise,' said Gramps.

Timmy looked up again. It wasn't just any old lady up a ladder. It was May! Timmy ran up the road to greet her. Slowly, carefully balancing her paint pot in one hand, May climbed down to the pavement.

'What are you doing here?' said Timmy, throwing his arms around her.

'I couldn't keep away,' she smiled. 'I realised there was more for me here than in the States. Do you think you could put up with me again, Timmy?'

'Yes, yes, yes,' said Timmy. And Gramps stood there with a twinkle in his eye.

18

For the first time, Timmy felt sorry for Mickey the Moose and pity was a better feeling than fear, for it gave Timmy strength. There was nothing to be frightened of, after all. Mickey was just a small bully fish being bullied by a much bigger, scarier bully fish.

On Monday Mickey had to take a lot of stick from the rest of the boys and girls at school for having lost the football match. Timmy watched as they taunted him, calling him Mickey the Mouse. Even his old friend and sidekick Freddy Hammer joined up with Fergus McNab and Charlie Holdgate to be horrid to him. No one was interested in bullying Timmy or Jason Dine. In Mickey, they had much better prey.

At break, it was Timmy who went to Mickey's rescue.

'It wasn't his fault,' he said to a bunch of older boys and girls. 'It was an accident. It could have happened to anyone.'

'What's that you're saying, nipper?' said one of the girls.

Timmy swallowed and said bravely, 'I'm just saying it could have happened to anyone.'

'Wait,' said Frank Hopp, who was Captain of the Over Tens, 'you're Timmy Twinkle, right?'

'Right,' said Timmy.

'Go on then, show us what you can do. Mr Daniels says you're a star, the best he's ever seen. Prove it.'

The older boys laughed until they saw Timmy play; the way he could make that ball spin and stay with him was a sight worth seeing.

'I tell you,' said Frank Hopp, 'if you were older, I'd have you on my team.'

Timmy tried not to show it, but he felt mighty chuffed.

At the end of school, Mickey was waiting for Timmy outside the school gates. For a moment Timmy's stomach lurched. Oh no, he thought, this is trouble. Then an

image of the mountain of a man came to him and he stopped feeling frightened.

'Hey, you,' said Mickey.

Timmy stopped walking and stared at him.

'Just want to say,' mumbled Mickey, 'thanks for butting in like that.'

'That's OK,' said Timmy.

'Good,' said Mickey, and walked off quickly.

The next match was against St John's School. Gramps brought May along to watch. Mickey's dad had been banned from the match, so just his mum came. She watched and only cheered when the other parents did.

This time the team played well together. Timmy scored three goals, Mickey one. And for the first time ever, Timmy felt that he and Mickey were playing on the same team.

19

It was after three schools had complained about High Hope football team, saying that nobody stood a chance against a striker like Timmy Twinkle, that a newspaper reporter picked up on the story. The headline read, 'The boy with the lightning feet.' There was a picture of Timmy making the ball spin, and below were comments from other sports teachers who had watched Timmy play.

'It's not an even playing field when they have Timmy Twinkle on their side,' said Mr Robinson, who was sports master at St

Cuthbert's. 'That boy can score from anywhere. He's unstoppable.'

Certain parents from other schools said that Timmy shouldn't be allowed to play in the Cup Final.

'It doesn't do the boys any good if one of them is so much better than the rest,' said Mrs Jones, head of City Academy Parents' Support Group. 'My son Jonas is feeling defeated. He was always thought of as a good striker until that Timmy Twinkle scored twelve goals against the Academy last week.'

'A load of tosh,' said Mr Daniels, scrunching up the paper. 'What's wrong with people?'

High Hope School was very proud of Timmy's achievements and even the headmaster entered into the debate. *The Herald* newspaper which had first published the article about Timmy was so taken with the story that they ordered new football kit for the team to wear. Their shirts had 'High Hope sponsored by *The Herald*' printed on the back.

Now the thing about newspapers is that they get read by everybody and although it was just a local paper, that hadn't stopped James Fenton, a scout for Arsenal, from reading it. He had been visiting an aunt outside London and had bought the paper to read on the train. The story about Timmy Twinkle, the boy with the lightning feet, had interested him a lot. He'd phoned Mr Daniels to ask when he could see Timmy play.

'At the Cup Final,' said Mr Daniels with pride.

The Cup Final was against Martha Ellis School. They had had a very good last season and were thought to be about equal with High Hope. But that was before High Hope had Timmy on their side.

20

It was raining on the day of the match, and the field was more like a mudbath than a football pitch. Up to now, Timmy had only played on dry surfaces, for there had hardly been any rain that autumn. Timmy was unsure of the ground. Mickey was unsure about his dad who wasn't going to take no for an answer and was determined to see his son play.

'As long as you're quiet,' said Mr Daniels firmly to the mountain of a man.

'No one says that when I go to watch Arsenal,' said the man crossly.

'This,' said Mr Daniels curtly, 'is the school's Cup Final match for the Under Tens.'

The mountain of a man sat himself down, or rather propped himself up, on a walking stick that had a sort of seat at one end. At least he can't get stuck, thought Timmy.

The team names were called out and with pats on the back from the parents and loads of clapping they ran out and took their places. The two captains came forward and the ref flipped a coin. Martha Ellis won the toss and the game started.

It was like being on an ice rink. Timmy seemed to be skating round all over the place. He suddenly felt very self-conscious.

The faces in the crowd all seemed to be watching him, just him, and he knew his mind wasn't on the game. He felt his confidence drain out of his football boots as the Martha Ellis defender tackled him easily, taking the ball.

Timmy slipped, tried to straighten up and fell hard on the ground. Suddenly there seemed to be a wall of sound coming from the other side as Martha Ellis scored the first goal.

Timmy stood up. He had cut his knee. Then he heard one boy shout out, 'Useless, useless! Fatty Batty's useless!'

The cry was taken up by others.

'I can do this, I can do this,' said Timmy, trying to encourage himself. His knee was bleeding as he kicked the ball way too clumsily and way too high. It soared over the top of the goal.

'Useless, useless!' came the chant.

In the next five dreadful minutes Martha Ellis scored another goal. Two nil. Now Timmy felt that everyone was looking at him and everyone was talking about him, chitter-chatter, chitter-chatter, chitter-chatter.

He felt a big empty ache inside him. What was happening? Where was his sparkle? Where was his twinkle? His feet felt like bricks.

Mickey seemed to be much happier playing on a muddy pitch. His movements stopped the ball in its tracks and he even managed to make one excellent header, missing the goal by inches.

'That's my lad,' shouted the mountain of a man, 'that's my boy!'

By the end of the first half, Timmy still hadn't scored. He felt totally defeated.

'Are you all right?' asked Jason.

'No,' said Timmy miserably. 'I'm useless.'

'No, you're not,' said Jason. 'Come on, man. You can do this. You know you can.'

Mickey ran up, slurping at his water bottle. 'Why haven't you scored?' he said.

'I don't know,' said Timmy, feeling desperate. 'I've lost my lightning feet.'

'You can't have done,' said Jason. 'Not now, not here.'

'I'll try to pass it to you more,' said Mickey.

'Thanks,' said Timmy, 'but it's no good. I'm just useless.'

'Very funny,' said Mr Daniels, walking up to Timmy. He looked furious. 'What are you playing at, Twinkle? I'd like you to know there's a scout here from Arsenal. Came all the way to see you, but for what? Are you trying to make me a laughing stock?'

'No, sir,' said Timmy, 'it's just –'

'It's just what?' said Mr Daniels, stuffing his fists into his tracksuit bottoms for want of something to do with them.

'Sir,' said Mickey.

'What?' snapped Mr Daniels.

'It'll be all right, sir. I'm sure it will,' said Mickey.

'So you can see into the future now, Morris,' said Mr Daniels.

'No, sir,' said Mickey, 'but Timmy's never let us down. He'll pull something out of the bag. I know it.'

Mr Daniels stormed off without another word.

The whistle blew and everyone took up their positions. Timmy was about to put his water bottle down by the bench and go back on to the field when, to his surprise, he saw the lad in the old-

fashioned clothes standing next to him.

'Timmy Twinkle, listen to me,' said the lad. 'This is really important. I know how you're feeling, but it's going to change. Seize your power. Remember all the things I taught you. Don't be defeated. Be hungry to win. You can do it!'

He stood there all golden like the end of a great summer's day.

'You won't be seeing me again,' the lad went on. 'You won't need to. You're going to win this cup and many more besides, Timmy Twinkletoes.'

Timmy stood staring as he began to fade away.

'Uncle Vernon?' he called, but it was too late. The lad had gone.

The whistle blew and brought Timmy back to here and now.

'What are you waiting for, Twinkle?' shouted the ref.

21

Football is a game of two halves, and it's a good thing it is, for in the second half Timmy found what he had lost to mud and nerves in the first. He went for the ball as if possessed, and from a distance scored the first of four goals. When the second goal shot through the goalie's legs there was a huge 'Whoopee!' from the crowd. The third was a rocket from the halfway line. Each goal was scored with a power and accuracy that flummoxed the onlookers.

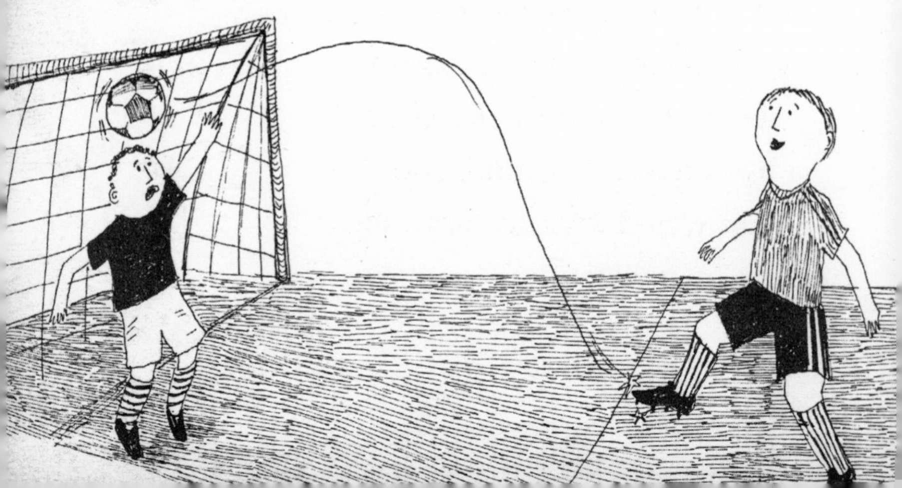

By now, the rain had turned to drizzle. Timmy didn't even notice.

James Fenton, the Arsenal scout, had been watching the match from the side. He had been about to give up and call it a day at the end of the first half. How many games like this had he been made to watch because some parent or sports teacher had wittered on about having found the next football legend! 'In their dreams,' thought James Fenton bitterly.

He'd only stayed because two other boys in the team showed promise. Otherwise he would have got back into his BMW and driven home. Now he was more than glad he hadn't left. What Mr Daniels had said was an understatement. Timmy Twinkle's feet hardly seemed to touch the ground, and the ball was drawn to him as if by magnets.

He watched as Timmy weaved and moved, ducked and dived, tricking players this way and that before shooting goals. The article in the paper was right. No one stood a chance against this boy. The final goal came from Timmy from almost the other side of the pitch, about as far away as you can get. The crowd roared and James Fenton knew he'd found himself a star.

Some people said it could have only been a fluke, but Timmy knew it wasn't. So did Mr Daniels. Martha Ellis School, players and supporters, looked utterly dejected as Timmy was carried round the pitch by his team-mates.

They all had their pictures taken. Mr Daniels got a bottle of ginger ale and poured it in the Cup, saying that was what they did when professionals won a game.

He said it was usually done with champagne, but seeing as they were all under ten, they'd better stick to pop.

'Eh, well done, lad,' said Gramps, rushing on to the pitch with May to hug Timmy.

Timmy looked round to see Jason's dad patting him on the back and looking as proud of his son as any dad could. Only Mickey stood apart, looking frightened of his dad.

'Why didn't you score, you idiot? Why'd you let that other boy take over?' he shouted. 'Yet again, you've let me down!'

Mickey just hung his head.

'Would it be all right if I asked Mickey back to tea too, with Jason?' asked Timmy.

'That's a grand idea,' said Gramps.

22

May had hung the teashop with flags and laid a table with a white cloth and a tea to be proud of. They were just about to sit down when the doorbell rang.

'Who can this be?' said Gramps, getting up to answer it.

Howdy,' called Sheriff as Mr Daniels and James Fenton came into the teashop.

'Good to see you both. Sit down and join the party,' said Gramps.

The boys looked very surprised to see the visitors and Mickey wondered if he'd done something wrong.

'No lad,' laughed James Fenton, 'you've done well. I've a little proposition for you three boys. I want you,' he said, pointing to Mickey and Jason, ' to come for trials at Arsenal.'

Mickey and Jason's mouths fell open.

'Are you sure?' said Mickey.

'Do you really mean us?' said Jason.

'Yes,' said James Fenton. 'If it hadn't been for you two, I would have left after the first half. Then I would never have got to see young Master Twinkle play.' Here, he cleared his throat. 'Timmy,' he said, 'we're offering you a place on a trainee programme at Arsenal to play for the Junior Gunners.'

'Me? You want me?' said Timmy.

'Eh, lad,' said Gramps, 'you look as if you've been hit over the head with a wet kipper.'

'But what about trials?' asked Timmy.

'No, lad,' said James Fenton. 'With your gifts, no trials are needed. We want you outright.'

Timmy stood still, hardly able to believe what he had just heard.

'Oh my, that is just wonderful,' said May, breaking the silence. 'Why, that's what you've been dreaming of, Timmy.'

A huge cheer went up around the room.

'This calls for something special,' said Gramps, disappearing into the kitchen. He reappeared with a cake that he'd iced like a football pitch with goals at either end, plus a little figure of a goalkeeper and two other players. In the centre of the cake was written 'Twinkletoes.'

'These,' said Timmy, pointing to the figures, 'are my best mates. Here's Jason in goal. And this one is Mickey,'

Mickey gave an enormous grin and then everyone started talking nineteen to the dozen.

'Did you really mean that?' Mickey asked Timmy as the cake was being cut.

'Yep,' said Timmy.

'You're a good mate,' said Mickey, smiling.

'We're a good team,' said Jason.

The three boys burst out laughing.

'Who'd have thought it!' said Timmy.

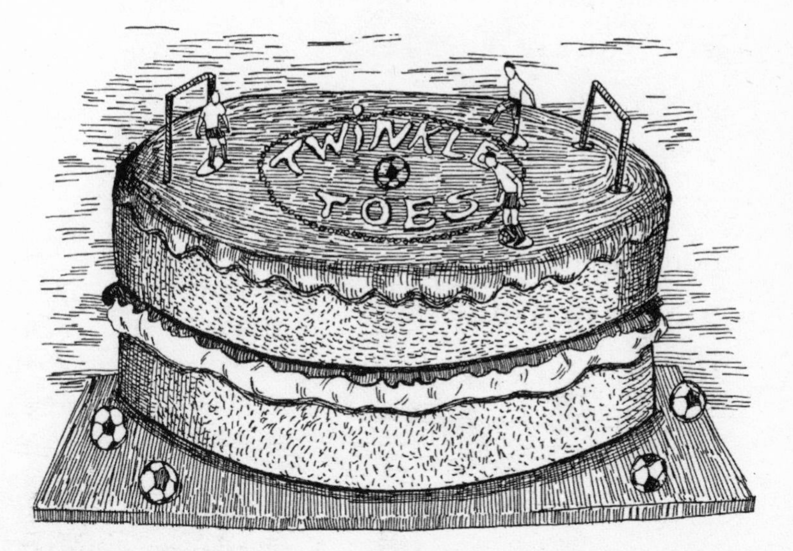

Footnote:

Both Mickey and Jason got through the trials to join Timmy at Arsenal.

May married Gramps and they opened up the teashop again. May ran Keep Fit classes upstairs.

'Honey,' she'd say to Gramps, 'let them eat cake, as long as they exercise.'

As for Timmy Twinkle, all I can say is keep your eye out. You never know. One day he may be using his lightning feet to win the World Cup.